C000192631

catherine
Wells

Gilbert
and the
Birthday Cake

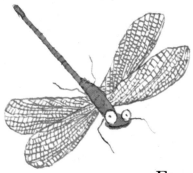

For my mother. J.H.
For Gilbert Spurling. A.T.

Hutchinson Children's Books Ltd

An imprint of Century Hutchinson Ltd
Brookmount House, 62–65 Chandos Place, Covent Garden, London WC2N 4NW

Hutchinson Publishing Group (Australia) Pty Ltd
16–22 Church Street, Hawthorn, Melbourne, Victoria 3122, Australia

Hutchinson Group (NZ) Ltd
32–34 View Road, PO Box 40–086, Glenfield, Auckland 10

Hutchinson Group (SA) Pty Ltd
PO Box 337, Bergvlei 2012, South Africa

First published 1986
© Ann Thwaite 1986
Illustrations © Jack Harvey 1986

Set in 16/18 Baskerville
Printed and bound in Great Britain

British Library Cataloguing in Publication Data

Thwaite, Ann
Gilbert and the birthday cake.
I. Title   II. Harvey, Jack *1953–*
823'.914[J]   PZ7

ISBN 0 09 162430 4

HUTCHINSON
London   Melbourne   Auckland   Johannesburg

Gilbert
and the
Birthday Cake

Jack Harvey & Ann Thwaite

Gilbert lived in the marshes on the edge of
a wide pond, with his family and all their
friends and relations. He was not much
good at hopping but he owned a red
bicycle which made him very happy.

One day his mother said to him, 'It is your grandfather's birthday. I have ordered a splendid cake for him. Will you please cycle to the station, take a train to the city and collect it from the baker's in Frogman's Walk.'

She gave him the money and a box to fit on the back of his bike. 'You are the only frog with a bicycle and the only one who can be entrusted with this important task,' she said.

Gilbert cycled to the station.

He padlocked his bike to the railings and
bought his return ticket from the crocodile
in the booking office.

Gilbert liked trains. He liked watching the
countryside speed by the windows.

Gilbert liked listening to the talk of his
fellow passengers and guessing what they
had eaten for breakfast.

He liked reading a book without his
brothers and sisters interrupting him.

When the train stopped at the city station, Gilbert got out and hopped the short distance to Frogman's Walk.

'And what can I do for you?' asked the badger in the baker's shop. 'We have a very nice line in currant buns.'

'No, thank you,' said Gilbert, though he liked currant buns. 'I have come for my grandfather's birthday cake.'

'Ah, you must be Gilbert,' the baker said. 'I have your grandfather's birthday cake ready for you. And a very splendid cake it is too, though I say so myself.'

He fitted the cake into Gilbert's box. Gilbert used his book to wedge it so it couldn't move around.

'There you are, young frog,' said the badger. And he gave Gilbert a currant bun to eat on the journey.

Gilbert walked down the road holding the box carefully.
He felt very proud to be carrying such a splendid cake.

When he got into the train for his return journey, he took his book out, and put the box, with the cake in it, very carefully on the luggage rack.

Then he settled down to eat his bun and
read his book.

The countryside sped by. They went
through several stations. The ticket
collector took Gilbert's ticket. 'Next stop,
young frog,' he said.

Gilbert went on reading his book.

Suddenly, the train stopped. Gilbert had been so engrossed in his book he hadn't realized they were coming to the station. He leapt up, hopped along the corridor, opened the door and jumped out on to the platform, clutching his book.

It was only when he had reached his bicycle that he realized his box with the splendid birthday cake in it was still on the train.

Gilbert rushed back to the platform. The train was disappearing into the distance.

What could he do?

Gilbert knew that the next station, where the train stopped for the night, was five miles away.

He simply couldn't return home without the splendid birthday cake.

So he decided to ride his bicycle all the
way to the end of the railway line to rescue
the cake.

Gilbert set off on his long ride.

Up hills and down again, Gilbert rode as
fast as he could, facing all the hazards of
the journey with amazing courage. He was
determined to make up for his terrible
carelessness in forgetting the precious
birthday cake.

But would he ever see it again? There was
the chance that some unscrupulous fellow
traveller had taken it home for an
unbirthday tea.

At last Gilbert saw the end of the
railway line in the distance.

LOST
PROPERTY

UNCLAIMED PERISHABLES MAY BE CONSUMED BY STATION STAFF

As he arrived at the station Gilbert saw a large notice on one of the buildings.

LOST PROPERTY

it said, and in smaller letters underneath:

UNCLAIMED PERISHABLES MAY BE CONSUMED BY STATION STAFF.

Gilbert's heart was beating very fast. He knew that a birthday cake was perishable. He knew that 'consumed' meant 'eaten'. Was he in time to save his grandfather's splendid cake?

He pushed open the door and peered inside.

Six of the station staff, relaxing at the end of their day's work, were gathered round a table. One had a box of matches to light the candles. Another had a knife in his hand, ready to cut the first slice.

Gilbert was *just* in time. 'I claim my grandfather's lost birthday cake,' he shouted.

Gilbert arrived home as it was getting
dark. Everyone was waiting for him.

'It's Gilbert!' they shouted as he walked
through the door.

'*And* the birthday cake,' said his mother.

'Happy birthday, Grandfather,' said
Gilbert, putting the splendid birthday
cake on the table.

That night old grandfather frog and all
the other animals had the best birthday
party that had ever been held in the
marshes.